Mental
Fight

Mental Fight

Ben Okri

PHOENIX HOUSE
London

Mental Fight is based on 'A Moment
in Timelessness', first delivered as the
inaugural millennium lecture sponsored
by the *Scotsman* at the 1997 Edinburgh
Book Festival. In its present form, the
first two sections were first published
in the *Times* in January 1999.

First published in Great Britain in 1999 by Phoenix House

A CIP catalogue record for this book
is available from the British Library.

ISBN 1 861591 64 0

Typeset by Deltatype Ltd,
Birkenhead, Merseyside
Printed by Clays Ltd, St Ives plc

Phoenix House
An imprint of the Weidenfeld & Nicolson division of
The Orion Publishing Group Ltd
Orion House
5 Upper Saint Martin's Lane
London, WC2H 9EA

An anti-spell for
The twenty-first century

To Humanity in the Aquarian Age

I will not cease from Mental Fight
Nor shall my Sword sleep in my hand
Till we have built Jerusalem

William Blake

ONE
Time to be real

I

An illusion by which we can become
More real.
A moment unremarked by the universe,
By nature, the seasons, or stars.
Moment we have marked out
In timelessness.
Human moment.
Making a ritual, a drama, a tear
On eternity.
Domesticating the infinite.
Contemplating the quantum questions,
Time, death, new beginnings,
Regeneration, cycles, the unknown.

II

Allow uncontemplated regions
Of time to project themselves
Into your sleeping consciousness,
Inducing terror, or mental liberation.
Much as death-confrontation
Paralyses some with despair
Makes others poison
Themselves with emptiness
But releases in a fortunate few
A quality of enlightenment
A sense of the limited time we have
Here on earth to live magnificently
To be as great and happy as we can
To explore our potential to the fullest
And to lose our fear of death
Having gained a greater love
And reverence for life
And its incommensurable golden brevity.

So it is with this moment.
A gigantic death
And an enormous birth.
This mighty moment.
In timelessness.

III

Illusions are useful only if we use them
To help us get to our true reality.
Initiations and rituals, if they are noble,
Have this power,
(They magnify the secret hour)
They enable us to pass from
The illusion of our lesser selves
To the reality of our greater selves,
Our soaring powers.
They free us from our smallness,
'Our humiliated consciousness', as Camus said,
And they deliver us
Into what we really are
What we sometimes suspect we are
What we glimpse we are when in love,
Magnificent and mysterious beings
Capable of creating civilisations
Out of the wild lands of the earth
And the dark places in our consciousness.

We are, in ways small and great,
The figures, the myths and legends
That we ourselves have invented.
Our dreams are self-portraits.
Our myths, our heroic legends,
Are the concealed autobiography
Of the human race
And its struggles
Through darkness to light
And through higher darkness again.

IV

Human kind cannot live long
With the notion
Or the reality
Of timelessness.
Only in the mind.
Only in the spirit.

With us, things must have a beginning.
Theatre grew from ritual,
And ritual grew out of the silence.
Here, now, is an origin.
We are poised always at the threshold
Of an unknown, unwritten, unforeseen act.
Let's gather ourselves together,
Clear our minds,
Make ourselves present to ourselves
And to our age.
That we be focussed
On this stage.
That we concentrate.
And listen.
That we prepare ourselves
In seriousness
And with joy.
Let's be wonderfully awake
For what we are going to create,
To make happen,
In this mass co-scripting
Of the future.

V

Now is a material event.
It is also a spiritual moment.
And the blinding light of the real
Can pierce through and tear
Asunder the unreal.
Every moment thus carries
The ordinary and the monumental:
Staring out of an office window
Or being blinded, like Paul,
On the plain road to Damascus,
By the light of true seeing.
Then the celluloid of what seems
Like the real world
Is stripped away.
And behind it all we see things
As they could be.
A better world, new, a world renewed.
This moment is thus,
It carries dust and dreams
Pavement or streams.
A moment on the clock
Or a moment of the spirit.
I dream of what it can be
I dream of what this
Millennial moment can be,
What we could let it be:

A wonderful excuse for beginning
A clearing out of the garbage
In our histories and our consciousness.
Best excuse in a thousand years
To transcend our grim ancient fears.

VI

Everyone loves a Spring cleaning.
Let's have a humanity cleaning.
Open up history's chamber of horrors
And clear out the skeletons behind the mirrors,
Put our breeding nightmares to flight
Transform our monsters with our light.
Clear out the stables
In our celebrated fables
A giant cleaning
Is no mean undertaking.
A cleaning of pogroms and fears
Of genocide and tears
Of torture and slavery
Hatred and brutality.
Let's turn around and face them
Let's turn around and face them
The bullies that our pasts have become
Let's turn around and face them
Let's make this clearing-out moment
A legendary material atonement.

TWO
Signs from the old times

I

O the hallucinations that can fall upon you
When you resist revelation,
When you resist epiphanies,
When you close yourself
Off from enlightenment.
The opposite of a spiritual dawn
Is a universal nightmare.
Then the mind multiplies
The illusion of things
Till they become not gods,
But god-like monsters.

O the nightmare visions
Of Breughel and Bosch,
The infernos of druggies
The neurotic hades
Are but the mental productions
Of illusions gone utterly wrong.
Apocalyptic visions are of great value.
They show us what the world
Will be like if we don't
Open ourselves to the other side,
To light, to freed thinking.
They are moral signposts
On the way to hell.

II

What will we choose?
Will we allow ourselves to descend
Into universal chaos and darkness?
A world without hope, without wholeness
Without moorings, without light
Without possibility for mental fight,
A world breeding mass murderers
Energy vampires, serial killers
With minds spinning in anomie and amorality
With murder, rape, genocide as normality?
Or will we allow ourselves merely to drift
Into an era of more of the same
An era drained of significance, without shame,
Without wonder or excitement,
Just the same low-grade entertainment,
An era boring and predictable
'Flat, stale, weary and unprofitable'
In which we drift
In which we drift along
Too bored and too passive to care
About what strange realities rear
Their heads in our days and nights,
Till we awake too late to the death of our rights
Too late to do anything
Too late for thinking
About what we have allowed
To take over our lives
While we cruised along in casual flight
Mildly indifferent to storm or sunlight?

III

Or might we choose to make
This time a waking-up event
A moment of world empowerment?
To pledge, in private, to be more aware
More playful, more tolerant, and more fair
More responsible, more wild, more loving
Awake to our unsuspected powers, more amazing.

We rise or fall by the choice we make
It all depends on the road we take
And the choice and the road each depend
On the light that we have, the light we bend,
On the light we use
Or refuse
On the lies we live by
And from which we die.

IV

Every moment thus carries
The monumental in the ordinary,
Transcending the political
Hinting at the evolutionary.

Great sudden leaps of consciousness,
Spontaneous descents into atavism
Might all seem revolutionary
But they are merely the seeds,
Long hidden in the earth,
Bursting forth into shoot.
They are merely the moments
In which what was hidden
Growing unseen in history's depths,
Suddenly combusts, brings forth its truest forms,
Revealing its real nature.
The speed and suddenness of an appearance
Is really only that moment
When we become aware
Of the change in a condition
(As in an enchanter's invocation)
A change that has been changing
All along, without our being aware of it.

V

And so under the powerful sun
And fertile intensity of this great moment
Many thoughts, forms, philosophies,
Regressions, advancements, tendencies,
Many hybrids, fusings, contortions,
And startling, sinister combinations
Pour out noisily
From the weird oracles of humanity.
A tidal wave of them.
Many things and signs
From the old times
Speed forth to fruition
Born too quickly
Too violently, too silently
The world aquiver with peculiar spawns
Born into early sunlight and harsh dawns.

And there would be too many gods
Too many Delphis
An unholy babbling
All over the narrow spaces.

Everywhere an excess of dreams,
Of forebodings, of art forms,
Of rituals, and ways, and interpretations,
Of roads, and signs and wonders,
Of prognostications, and wayward visions.
Babel is rebuilt amongst us.
Babel is reborn.

VI

We know only two kinds of response
To the unknown.
Awe, or noise;
Silence, or terror;
Humility, or paralysis;
Prayer, or panic;
Stillness, or speech;
Watchfulness, or myth-making;
Seeing clearly, or inventing what we see;
Standing, or fleeing;
Reasoning, or falling apart;
Courage, or cowardice.

The unknown lives with us
Lives in each moment.
Like a new millennium,
The unknown is as richly potent
As the critical mass
Of our mass minds
Facing the momentous.

Humanity is at its most radioactive.
Fusing and fissioning.
Giving off energies abundant
Like so many little solar systems.
Hurling out so many seeds,
Like the fertile season in great forests.
Out of these energies,
Out of time's sifting,
Will come a new future,
Unrecognisable to those of us who live
And breathe now.

And out of so many seeds,
(Innumerable deeds,)
Will come a new humanity
Which will owe much
To this point of the cusp,
To this moment in which we live,
To now, here, as we move
Towards flowing future time
That bears us ever onwards
Into eternity.

We are the best placed farmers
Of new time.
We are at a precious moment
In time's ovulation.

We are now at that rare intersection
That magic favours,
That history adores,
That legend has no need to embellish
Because it is already a legendary moment
In its own wonderful right.

VII

How often have great minds
In the past prayed, and wished
For better favoured moments
In time to unleash their best
Gifts on humanity?
This is one such conjunction:
It fills the heart with too much humility
And amazement to behold.
But we must behold it, with minds calm,
With aspirations clear,
And with the smile in the soul
That only those fortunate people have
Who find themselves at the right time,
At the perfect mythic conjunction
That is also a living moment.
A moment lived through.

We are living in enchanted time.
With our spirits right
We can enchant the future.
With our love's might
We can give a truer meaning to our past.

I

Is time exhausted?
No, time is yet young,
And has timeless millennia ahead,
Way beyond our furthest dreams.

Is nature exhausted?
Ask the oak-trees, the hollies,
The flowers, birds, fishes, and lions.
They will continue for as long
As the earth allows them.

Is humanity exhausted?
Individuals are, nations are,
Some civilisations are becoming so;
But humanity isn't.

The hungry nations are hungry still.
The starving people dream of food.
The unfree fight for freedom.
The oppressed plan for liberation.
The small scheme for might.
The invisible prepare for higher visibility.

They are only exhausted
Who think they are.
They are only exhausted who no longer
Have a reason to strive
And dream and hope.

They are only exhausted who think
That they have arrived
At their final destination,
The end of their road,
With all of their dreams achieved,
And with no new dreams to hold.

The exhausted are those who have
Come to the end of their powers
Of imagination, who have limited
Their possibilities, who have thought
Themselves into the dead ends
That they call the highest
Points of their civilisations.

Those who are exhausted have lost
The greater picture,
The greater perspective.
They are trapped in their own labyrinth,
Their lovelessness, selfishness.
For those with limited dreams,
There is chaos to come.
Disintegration. Nightmares.

I hear them talk about the end
Of history.
But those of us who haven't tasted
The best fruits of time yet,
To whom history has been harsh,
We think differently.
We know that history is all there
To be made in the future.

Exhaustion is a mental thing,
The absence of a spiritual viewpoint,
A universal vision,
A sense of new journeys,
Higher discoveries.

There is no exhaustion where there is much
To be hoped for, much to work towards,
And where the dreams and sufferings
Of our ancestors
Have not been realised,
Or redeemed.

There is no exhaustion
When you can still visualise
A better life for those who suffer.
Visualise universal justice.
A leavening of the great dough
Of humanity.
Uplifting the multitudes.

But when you can no longer dream
No longer see possibilities
No longer see alternatives;
When you can see only limitation
Only despair, and negation,
Then you are in the way.
You are also the problem.
The exhausted obstruct
The creation of a greater future.

The exhausted should therefore clear
The stage for new dreamers –
For warriors of love, justice,
And enlightenment.

II

Have all thoughts, possibilities, ideas,
Philosophies been exhausted?
Has Christianity found its fullest
Fruition in great cathedrals, charities,
Schisms, wars, orthodoxies,
And sundry creeds?
I do not believe that Christianity
Has yet yielded ailing humanity
Its best fruits. Unrealised remain
Her fullest possibilities.

Have Buddhism, Taoism, Hinduism,
Islam, Humanism and Existentialism
All the spiritual aspirations of the race
All thoughts of social organisation
All ideas technological and scientific –
Have they all been richly realised
Fully mined and made to serve
And ennoble and feed humankind?
I don't think so either.
Look at history and see what you find.

FOUR

The stony ground

I

Humanity has been so much like a child
With too many useful toys,
Playing with each one that comes along,
And discarding it when something
Newer appears in its midst.

We have been dilettantes and amateurs
With some of our greatest notions
For human betterment.
We have been like spoilt children:
We have been like tyrannical children;
We have been impatient and imperious
Demanding proof when listening is required,
Tearing things down when they don't do
What we want them to do
(How much simpler to let things do only
What they can do)
Being uncreative about what seems dark
And terrifying;
Preferring only what seems easy
And effortless;
Asking about the numbers of a philosophy's
Followers rather than examining
The efficacy of its ideas;

Wandering down blind alleys of populism
That lead to concentration camps;
Refusing to admit our vast crimes and mistakes
Denying the horrors of the slave trade
Minimising the reality of the gas chambers
Tearing our hair out in futile attempts
To reconcile civilisation with genocide,
When civilisation (as we have come to accept it)
Never did mean true universal goodness
Of heart, but rather the self-mythology
Of a people, a race.
No, neither the good in us
Nor our capacity for evil are exhausted.
And time will show just how young
We are in our abilities,
Our genius for good and evil.
For all these strains, unexamined, unredeemed,
Will find their higher fruition
In the unlit centuries to come.

We carry with us, across the silver river
Of the new age, many ambiguous
And deadly seeds,
And many seeds of illumination too.
We are the sum total of the history
That we have not truly examined.
We are the carriers of history's
Future diseases or cures.
The sooner we face the spawn
We carry within us in silence
The better it will be.
The sooner we admit our crimes to others,
To other peoples, creeds, genders, species,
The better and lighter the human
Future will be.
The more we deny, the greater will be the horrors
And vengeances of time
That wait silently in the wings
Of the bloody drama of our future.

Many beautiful thoughts have not yet sprouted
In our deepest hearts and minds,
Though they have lain there, within us,
Lain waiting for thousands of years.
The heart of humanity can
Sometimes be a stony ground indeed.
We speak the good words,
But do not live them.
We perform the beautiful rituals,
But don't embody them.
We praise our capacity for reason,
But are unreasonably intolerant
Of other people's validity, and reasons.
We deploy the finest attributes
Of the mind and spirit
To make ourselves the elect
And to cast our fellow travellers
On this earth into outer darkness.

What a wonder is humanity:
How marvellous its astonishing gift
For hypocrisy.

II

How healthy is the human race?
When the foot is swollen, the kidney ailing,
The neck stiff, the spirit troubled,
The heartbeat irregular, the head stuffy,
The thoughts narrow and negative,
But the whole taken together
Generally functional,
Can we say that the body is healthy?
So it is with humanity.

These are some of the illnesses of the race:
Tyranny, starvation, religious and tribal wars,
Repression, poverty, alienation, genocide,
Indifference, xenophobia, illiteracy,
Bad governments, epidemics, selfishness.
We must face the fact that
Given the whole picture
The human race is not that well.

We have also, it cannot be denied,
Accomplished great feats.
We have journeyed to space and spied
On the solitude of uninhabited planets.
We have created mighty secular
And religious structures,
Made fabulous technological inventions,
Found cures for horrible diseases,
Solved some riddles of human genetics,
Probed the mysteries of the weather,
Shed light on aberrations of the mind,
Exploded the possibilities of communications,
And tapped the awesome ambiguous
Power of nuclear energy.

And yet, because of our pollutions,
Earth's fragile balance is askew.
Humanity dies in refugee camps,
Goes mad in ghettoes,
Is brutalised by bad governments,
And perishes in festering wars.

And yet hatreds boil away
For reasons of history
And for different interpretations
Of the same sacred texts
That preach universal love.

We are amazing:
So much gold has been revealed
In the human spirit.
So many wonderful philosophies
Of startling simplicity
Have been dreamt up and shared
Amongst us,
And yet we still live
As if in Plato's cave,
Watching the shadows
Of sufferings go past
As if they had nothing to do with us.
And yet we live as if these thoughts,
These dreams, these philosophies,
Had not been uttered,
And never been beneficial.

I contend that the human race
Has not yet reached
The true condition
Of civilisation.

Sure, the quality of life has been enriched
For many over the past centuries;
But true civilisation is much more
Than the technological progress
Or well-being of part of the human race.

What we have called civilisations
Are merely stages on the way
To true world civilisation.

FIVE

Harmony of politics and heart

I

Mastery of material problems:
No spiritual way can reconcile
Itself truthfully with the raw wound
Of starving multitudes.
We cannot use the word civilisation
As long as people die of starvation.
Those who do are cave-dwellers
Of the mind.

Transmutation of world-wide poverty
Will be the greatest alchemical
Feat of the dreaming age.
A basic pre-condition of civilisation
Is a world free of hunger.
Cannot be done by charity alone.
Symphony of rich and poor
Nations of the earth.
No them and us.
No self-satisfaction.
No superiority-thinking.
Harmony of politics and heart.
Rhythms of economics and art.
Improvisations on the theme of justice:
If the rich go on exploiting the poor
We are talking about cannibalism.
If the rich go on ignoring the poor
Absolute violence will be the music
To such deafness.

With all our vaunted glories
We are still largely humiliated
Beings on earth.
It's time we turned our formidable
Powers of heart and mind
To humanity's solvable problems –
Problems which have become accusations.

This earth is our brief home.
Let's put the human house in order
Let's tend the wild garden of humanity.
We are better than the sum total
Of our successes and failures.
The truth is that we haven't really tried,
We haven't really gone for it,
We haven't really striven
For a world of balance
And contentment.
We are like athletes
Who haven't really extended themselves.
We haven't found out what we are
Really capable of doing,
If we put our minds to it.
We are functioning below
Our potential for love,
Justice, and creating a good world.

SIX
Hold on to your sanity

I

At the end of powerful eras,
And at the birth of new ones,
Strange spirits spew up
In the world, in nature,
In the heavens, from our minds.
Turbulences rise from secret places
And underworlds of history,
From our guilt and denial,
From our wickedness and silence.
From the oppressed and the suppressed.
From our conscience.
Great cries and monstrous visions
Sound from humanity's
Forgotten oracles.
Visions of terminal horrors
And eruptions.

The force of new eras
Clashing with the old,
Like two seas with two
Contending powerful gods,
Unleash things strange to behold.
Collapsing structures multiply:
Superstitions and anomie,
Paranoia and mindless cults,
Conspiracy theories and supernatural
Terrors, suicides and murders,
Wars and fears and panic
Wreak havoc on the world.
And only those with substance,

Whose souls are earthed,
Whose eyes are clear,
Withstand it all.
And they pay an awkward price
For such clear-sightedness.
They will be alone,
But hopefully not as tragically
Alone as the noble family
In 'Satyricon' who, unable
To bear such sanity
In the midst of universal insanity,
Elect for stoic suicide.

So watch your minds.
Cling on to the soundest values.
These are severely testing times ahead,
More testing for the sane
Than for those perfectly in tune
With erupting contemporary anomie.

II

For we are living on the cusp
Of wonders and terrors.
Tensions flow beneath the age
Like great subterranean rivers.
Never before has humanity,
In such full consciousness,
Drifted towards so momentous
A moment in measured time.
Minor spirits come out to play
And create mischief at Halloween
And on Walpurgis night.
Major spirits might well be about
In the slipstream of a new age.

And so hold on to the best
Things of the awakened mind.
Only the most solid and intangible
Aspects of the human spirit
Can save us from succumbing
To the waves of panic
That engulf us temporarily.

We need to become adaptive mariners.
But when the waves pass,
When the silver line has been crossed,
And when we are safely over,
A new calm will descend upon us.
A profound time-change will settle
On us as we find ourselves
Not in a new land
But in a new time,
A new space.

And at first we will seem adrift
On a strange sea where fishes
No longer resemble what they used to be,
And where we are no longer
What we were,
Or thought we were.

And we will have become less,
Or more,
Depending on what we have
Brought with us
From the old time,
The old space.

Now is the moment to choose
What we are going to freight over.
We are going to need our sanity later.
It will have been tempered
And raised to such a pitch
That out of its higher power
Will come the next stage
Of the evolution
Of human consciousness.
A higher history.
The foundations of a new
Universal civilisation

SEVEN

No one is a loser

I

Our future is greater than our past.
So far we have mostly misapplied
The powers of the mind.
We have under-applied
The wonders of the human spirit.
The mind that created pyramids,
Warfare, great art, and science,
Has not yet reached maturity.
Everything we have done till now
Merely suggests the power of the human
Mind in its infancy.

We are not defined by our failures.
Rivers have changed their courses.
There are revolutions in the heavens,
Among the stars, all the time.
New worlds are constantly being born.
What we call civilisation
Is only ten years old
In the mind of an oak tree,
And a minute old
To a distant star.
Tradition doesn't have to weigh us down.
We weigh ourselves down with tradition,
With the past, with past failures,
Past forms, past perceptions.
We have made these things;
We can unmake them.
Every now and again the earth breaks
Its crust, and molten liquid

In its depths spews out,
Turns to rocks, and forms new islands.
The mind of humanity is such a force.
New worlds wait to be created
By free minds that can dream unfettered,
Without fear, turning obstacles
Into milestones towards luminous glories.
The new age is such a time
For such new births.
We can all re-dream the world, our lives.
But the conception must begin now.
The birth must begin now.
We should consecrate ourselves
To clearing the deadwood and stale thinking
And backward perceptions from our minds.
We should begin to think anew.
To prepare ourselves for a new air,
For a fuller future.
The preparation would be rewarding,
For we are each one of us saviours
And co-makers of the world we live in.
But we should begin now, here,
Among one another,
And in solitude.

II

We must not think ourselves victims,
Disadvantaged, held back –
Because of race, colour, creed,
Education, class, gender,
Religion, height, or age.
The world is not made of labels.
The world, from now on,
Will be made through the mind.
Through great dreaming, great loving
And masterly application.
Those who transcend their apparent limitations
Are greater than those who apparently
Have little to transcend.
Our handicaps can be the seed of our glories.
We shouldn't deny them.
We should embrace them,
Embrace our marginalisation,
Our invisibility, our powerlessness.
Embrace our handicaps, and use them,
And go beyond them,
For they could well be the key
To some of the most beautiful energies
That we have been given.
Accept no limitations to our human potential.
We have the power of solar systems
In our minds.
Our rage is powerful.
Our love is mighty.
Our desire to survive is awesome.
Our quest for freedom is noble, and great.

And just as astonishing is the knowledge
That we are, more or less,
The makers of the future.
We create what time will frame.
And a beautiful dream, shaped
And realised by a beautiful mind,
Is one of the greatest gifts
We can make to our fellow beings.

III

Never again will we stand
On the threshold of a new age.
We that are here now are touched
In some mysterious way
With the ability to change
And make the future.
Those who wake to the wonder
Of this magic moment,
Who wake to the possibilities
Of this charged conjunction,
Are the chosen ones who have chosen
To act, to free the future, to open it up,
To consign prejudices to the past,
To open up the magic casement
Of the human spirit
Onto a more shining world.

Then, a few centuries into the future,
The miseries and the sufferings
Of continents will be the rumours
Of history;
There will be no famines
No mass starvations
No tolerance of tyranny
And liberty will have a more glorious song.
And then humanity will spend
Time's repletion dreaming of ways
To use the new freedoms and powers
Of the race for higher things,
Much as we find better uses
For electricity or solar energy.

EIGHT

Turn on your light

I

Do I see you recoil from such a vision?
Have we become so neck-deep
In cynicism that we threaten the race
With an ever-descending spiral
Of failure, inaction, negativity,
Indifference, boredom, and stupidity?
Cynicism only creates dead worlds;
Its symbol, devoid of beauty,
Is a deadland, where nothing grows.
That is not the smarter side
Of the human spirit, (as some would like to think),
But the smaller, meaner, least attractive,
The most death-encouraging side,
And the least effective.

We are better than that.
We are greater than our despair.
The negative aspects of humanity
Are not the most real and authentic;
The most authentic thing about us
Is our capacity to create, to overcome,
To endure, to transform, to love,
And to be greater than our suffering.
We are best defined by the mystery
That we are still here, and can still rise
Upwards, still create better civilisations,
That we can face our raw realities,
And that we will survive
The greater despair
That the greater future might bring.

II

The new era is already here:
Here the new time begins anew.
The new era happens every day,
Every day is a new world,
A new calendar.
All great moments, all great eras,
Are just every moment
And every day writ large.
Thousands of years of loving, failing, killing,
Creating, suprising, oppressing,
And thinking ought now to start
To bear fruit, to deliver their rich harvest.

Will you be at the harvest,
Among the gatherers of new fruits?
Then you must begin today to remake
Your mental and spiritual world,
And join the warriors and celebrants
Of freedom, realisers of great dreams.

You can't remake the world
Without remaking yourself.
Each new era begins within.
It is an inward event,
With unsuspected possibilities
For inner liberation.
We could use it to turn on
Our inward lights.
We could use it to use even the dark
And negative things positively.
We could use the new era
To clean our eyes,
To see the world differently,
To see ourselves more clearly.
Only free people can make a free world.
Infect the world with your light.
Help fulfill the golden prophecies.
Press forward the human genius.
Our future is greater than our past.

III

Already, the future is converging with the past.
Already the world is converging.
The diverse ways of the world
Will create wonderful new forms,
Lovely cultural explosions
In the centuries to come.
Already I sense future forms of art,
Of painting, sculpture, humour.
Already I sense future novels,
Plays, poems, dances.
Already I sense the great orchestras
Of humanity, a world symphony,
A world jam, in which the diverse
Genius of the human race –
Its rich tapestry of differences –
Will combine, weave, heighten,
Harmonise all its varied ways
And bring about a universal flowering
In all the vast numbers of disciplines
And among the unnumbered peoples.
Already I can hear this distant music
Of the future,
The magic poetry of time,
The distillation of all our different gifts.

It is all in the air.
It is all gathering in the underground
Coming together majestically.
We should listen to the things
Forming in the air,
The things forming in the underground.
We should do some deep serious working
On the spirit of the age
If we are going to bring about
A marvellous future,
If we are going to have some control
On how the unknown will affect us.
The air must be altered,
The underground must be understood,
For the overground to be different.

This distant music of the future
Haunts me.
And I think it will be something
Amazing to hear,
A delight to the gods,
Provided we don't lose our way
More than we already have,
And provided we are guided
By our deepest love,
The love that connects us all
On this little globe of beauty.

IV

And because we have too much information,
And no clear direction;
Too many facts,
And not enough faith;
Too much confusion,
And crave clear vision;
Too many fears,
And not enough light –
I whisper to myself modest maxims
As thought-friends for a new age.
  See clearly, think clearly.
  Face pleasant and unpleasant truths;
  Face reality.
  Free the past.
  Catch up with ourselves.
  Never cease from upward striving.
  We are better than we think.
  Don't be afraid to love, or be loved.
  As within, so without.
  We owe life abundant happiness.

V

The illusion of time will give way
To the reality of time . . .
And time present is made
Before time becomes present.
For all time is here, now,
In our awakening.

VI

For, after the gospels,
After the human and divine comedies,
After the one thousand and one nights,
After crime and punishment,
War and peace, pride and prejudice,
The sound and the fury,
Between good and evil,
Being and nothingness,
After the tempest, the trial,
And the wasteland,
After things have fallen apart,
After the hundred years of solitude,
And the remembrance of things past,
In the kingdom of this world,
We can still astonish the gods in humanity
And be the stuff of future legends,
If we but dare to be real,
And have the courage to see
That this is the time to dream
The best dream of them all.